The Suite Life of Zack & Cody

Hotel Hangout

Adapted by Kitty Richards

Based on the television series, "The Suite Life of Zack & Cody", created by Danny Kallis & Jim Geoghan

Based on the episode written by Jeny Quine

DISNEY PRESS

New York

Chapter 1

Zack and Cody Martin had a new home. An amazing new home, in fact. They were living in the Tipton, the swankiest hotel in all of Boston, Massachusetts. Their mother, Carey, had recently been hired as the singer in the hotel's ballroom. As part of her contract, she and her two sons got to live, rent free, in a suite on the twenty-third floor.

Zack and Cody were twins. They looked almost exactly alike—same height, same blond hair, same blue eyes. But it was easy to tell them apart because they were very different. Zack, as he liked to remind his brother as often as possible, was the oldest, by ten full minutes. He was the fun-loving brother, who liked to dress like a skateboarder in long shorts and cool shirts. Zack liked having fun, and he didn't mind if he got into trouble having it. It was almost impossible to get him to study, unless he was chained to his desk. Cody, on the other hand, was kind of preppy. He liked button-up shirts, vests, and sweaters. Cody was the more serious twin. He was better organized, studied harder, and took life a little more seriously than his twin.

Which twin was most likely to bring home an A-plus on his spelling test? Cody. Which twin was most likely to get in trouble for putting goldfish in the Tipton's sterling silver punch bowl? Zack.

But there was one thing that they both agreed on—living in the Tipton was totally awesome. Room service, a rooftop pool with a Jacuzzi, a candy counter in the lobby, a game room in the basement. If only they had some friends to share it with . . .

Today, the twins had decided, they were going to find themselves some friends at the park. There was just one problem—they had no way of getting there!

"Mom, why can't you drive us to the playground?" Cody asked for what seemed like the hundredth time that afternoon.

Carey sighed. "Because, I have to rehearse new choreography for my next show," she explained patiently. "Mr. Moseby thinks I need some younger moves."

Mr. Moseby was the manager of the Tipton Hotel, and he was also Carey's boss. He liked things in his hotel to be just so. And if he said that Carey needed some younger moves, then she needed to find some younger moves, pronto.

To illustrate her point, Carey attempted her version of a "younger move." Zack and Cody's mom may have looked hip with her choker, spiky hair, jeans, and high-heeled boots. But her moves were anything but. Doing a modified moonwalk across the lobby's polished floor, she spun her arms, looking like a spastic windmill. The boys winced.

"What do you think?" she asked her sons.

The boys didn't bother lying. "I think you should never do that in public," replied Zack.

"Or in private," added Cody.

Carey smiled at her boys. Then she

changed the subject. "Why don't you guys invite over some friends from school?" she suggested.

"That's a great idea!" said Cody sarcastically.

Zack rolled his eyes. "Too bad we don't *have* any. Nobody ever likes the new kids."

Carey looked sad for a moment, then brightened. "Come here," she said. She leaned over and kissed each twin on the cheek. "You'll make friends soon. We're here to stay now."

The boys grinned. "Not if you use those moves," replied Zack.

Zack began to imitate his mom's move, heading backward across the lobby. Waving his arms around, he accidentally knocked into the table by the hotel entrance. On that table sat a fancy Asian vase. Zack, Cody, and their mom stared in horror as the vase teetered and began to fall over. Just when it was about to crash to the floor, Esteban, the bellhop, made a spectacular diving catch and landed on his back, the vase safely in his arms. Saved by the bellhop!

Mr. Moseby rushed over. "Impressive catch, Esteban."

Esteban stood up. "If you thought that was impressive, Mr. Moseby, watch this." He flipped the vase in the air.

"Hey!" cried everyone in horror.

Esteban caught the vase and held it up to his ear like the world's largest conch shell. "Ooh, I can hear the ocean," he said with a wide grin.

"Let me hear! Let me hear!" Zack and Cody cried. They had forgotten all about the playground. Life at the Tipton tended to do that. There was always something going on to distract you!

Chapter 2

Maddie and London were like the twins—that is, *very* different. During the day, Maddie was a hardworking, down-to-earth, straight-A student. After school, she was a hardworking part-time employee of the Tipton Hotel, where she worked behind the candy counter and occasionally babysat Zack and Cody. Then there was London.

London Tipton, that is. Her father owned the hotel, and she lived in a lavish suite. London was a bit of a spoiled princess who loved clothes and accessories more than anything. The two girls pretended not to get along (and sometimes they actually didn't!), but despite their many differences, they really were good friends.

That evening, Maddie and London were chatting at the candy counter. Maddie was working, as usual, and London was about to go out, as usual. London was dressed to kill in pink pants, a silky patterned halter top, pink heels, sparkly pink hoop earrings, and an armful of gold bangles. Just then, Mr. Moseby walked up to the counter.

"London, I need to speak with you," he said.

"Not now, Moseby," said London. "I'm off to a gala premiere." She tucked her pink purse under her arm and strode off, only to find herself spinning back around when Mr. Moseby grabbed her arm.

"Oh, no, you're not," Mr. Moseby said seriously. "I just received a fax from your father. You are to cease all social activities until your grades improve." Mr. Moseby took his job very seriously, and spoke in a very no-nonsense manner. And he was especially serious about orders from his boss.

London's face fell. "That is *so* unfair! I have to keep my grades up, but his new wife is allowed to drop out of college?"

Mr. Moseby made a sympathetic face but didn't give up. "He also insisted I hire you a tutor."

London shook her head. "When is he going to realize that education and me just don't mix?"

Maddie, who was in the middle of ringing

up a sale, cleared her throat. "Education and 'I,'" she corrected.

London looked at her friend in disbelief. "Hello?" she said. "This isn't about *you*!"

Maddie rolled her eyes and turned back to her customer.

"Okay, that's nine dollars and twelve cents, minus your eight percent senior discount is . . ." she paused for a moment as she did the math in her head. "Eight dollars and thirty-eight cents. Out of ten," she said, accepting the bill. "One sixty-two is your change," she rattled off as the cash register spooled out the receipt. Maddie Fitzpatrick, human calculator!

Mr. Moseby couldn't believe his ears. He grabbed the receipt. "You beat the cash register!" He noticed a book on the counter and picked it up. "And you read!" he squealed. He turned to London and gestured toward

Maddie. "*Maddie* can be your new tutor."

Both London and Maddie's jaws fell open. "What?!" they cried.

Maddie shook her head. "There isn't enough money in the world," she pronounced, turning back to the register.

But Mr. Moseby wasn't letting the human calculator get away. "I'll pay you triple your salary," he responded.

Maddie thought for the briefest of moments, then turned to London. "Apparently there is enough!" she said.

❖❖❖

The next day after school, Zack and Cody were, as usual, by themselves in the school yard. They watched enviously as groups of kids walked by, laughing and joking. When were *they* going to make friends?

Just then Drew, the most popular kid in their class, walked by. Drew was tall and handsome. Today he was wearing his sweatshirt hood pulled up over his signature dreads. He was surrounded by his posse of friends, who followed him everywhere and did whatever he told them to do.

"Cody, check it out," Zack said. "It's the Drew Crew!" Before Cody could stop him from committing social suicide, Zack walked up to Drew. "Yo, Drew. What up, dawg?"

Drew gave the twins the once-over. "Hey look," he said scornfully. "It's the clones."

The Drew Crew laughed and moved on. Their job—humiliating the new kids—was done.

Zack was excited. "Did you hear that? The Drew Crew just mocked us!"

Cody sighed. It was amazing, the things his brother could get enthusiastic about.

"Whoo-hoo, we're in," he said sarcastically.

Just then the boys were approached by two kids—a tall skinny boy with wild brown hair and a short tomboy with big brown eyes, camo pants, and a baseball cap.

"The Drew Crew will never accept you. Don't beat your head against a wall," the tomboy told them. It was obvious she spoke from experience.

"Even though it feels good sometimes," offered the wild-haired boy helpfully.

The boys looked at each other. Huh? What was he talking about? The girl gave the tall kid an odd look, then shrugged it off. It was obvious that this wasn't the weirdest thing she'd ever heard him say.

"I'm Max, by the way," the girl said, pointing to herself. "And this is Tapeworm."

Zack stared. "What kind of name is that?" he asked.

Max made a face. "The kind you get when you eat twenty hot dogs in less than two minutes," she explained.

Cody nodded. "Cool, beats my record."

Zack stifled a laugh. "By *eighteen*!" he said. Cody gave Zack a look.

Zack ignored his brother, studying Max and Tapeworm. Kids were talking to them. And not making fun of them! He had a brilliant idea. "Hey, you guys wanna come over to our house?"

Tapeworm was thrilled. "Did you hear that? Someone wants us to come over to their house!"

Max grinned and nodded. The four headed off to the Tipton.

Zack and Cody could hardly believe their good fortune. They were finally making friends!

Chapter 3

When the kids arrived on the twenty-third floor of the Tipton Hotel, they walked into the most humiliating situation possible. Despite the twins' warning to never, ever practice her moves, even in private, their mom was doing just that. Just as they walked into the suite, she bent over and started dancing backward, shaking her finger and singing, "Ooh, and no, no, no . . ." into a hairbrush.

No was right! This dancing had to stop. Immediately!

Zack cleared his throat. "Mom!" he said warningly.

Carey looked up, startled. "Oh! Hey!" she said. She took her "mike" and ran it through her hair. As if that would fool anyone!

Cody's mouth was open in disbelief.

"Mom, what are you doing?" Zack asked.

Carey gave a fake laugh. "Apparently, I'm embarrassing myself." Then she finally noticed the two strangers. "In front of your new friends!" She rushed over to Max and Tapeworm and leaned over them a little too enthusiastically. "You made friends!"

Max leaned back, giving Carey a wary

look. "Maybe," she said, as she crossed her arms. Then she spotted the entertainment unit and ran over to it. "Whoa, this is so tight," she said approvingly. She pushed the PLAY button on the CD player and a hip-hop song came on. Max began moving to the music.

"I was just rehearsing for my new show," Carey started to explain. Then she took a look at Max. The girl could dance! "Man, look at you go!" Carey said. Max got so into it, her baseball cap fell off, revealing her braids. "Wow," Carey said. "Can you show me how you do that?"

"Sure," said Max, dropping to the floor in an elaborate break-dancing move. She spun around and then ended the routine with her legs in the air.

Carey crouched on the floor so that she and Max were face-to-face. "Okay. Now, the part a *mom* can actually do," she said.

"Oh, okay," said Max, still lying on the floor.

Things were looking better already. Not only did the kids have friends, but now Carey had a choreographer, too.

❖❖❖

Meanwhile, in the living room of London's lavish suite, filled with fresh-cut flowers in expensive vases, fancy lamps, mirrors, pictures in elaborate frames, and beautiful throw pillows, Maddie and London had embarked on the magical journey of learning. London, wearing a fashionable long brown tank with sequined straps, white pants, a jeweled choker, and a brand-new French manicure, was at her laptop.

"So, how's your research on Italy

coming?" Maddie asked brightly. She had changed out of her school uniform and was dressed in a light green sweater, green belt, mini–jeans skirt, and light green boots.

London beamed. "Fantastic!"

Maddie smiled, but only for a brief moment. London's next words put an end to Maddie's good mood.

"I had no idea Fabriuzzio sold dresses over the Internet!" London cried, pointing to the screen. "I'll order you one. What are you, a size fourteen?" she asked cluelessly.

"Yes, the same as your IQ," Maddie retorted. But her mind was on other things, and she quickly forgot the insult. She checked her watch. "Ooh, I have to get downstairs. He's probably there already," she said. She ran across the room, flailing her arms excitedly.

"Who's there?" said London, interested

despite herself. Now she knew why Maddie was so dressed up!

Maddie stopped at the door and spun around. "No one," she replied, trying to cover up, and doing it badly.

London ran across the room. "No one, who?" she wanted to know. "Is he cute?"

"It's nothing," said Maddie. But she couldn't hold back any longer. "Just the new lifeguard. He always buys gum before his shift. Spearmint," she added dreamily.

London grabbed Maddie's arm and tossed her down in a chair. She wanted details. Now! "Has he asked you out yet?" she asked intently.

"Not in so many words," replied Maddie. Then she corrected herself. "Or in any words, really." Then she opened up. "You know how it is when you really like a guy and he has no idea that you exist?"

London stared at Maddie blankly. "No," she said.

That was it. Maddie was done baring her soul. "I should go. I'm late." She stood up.

London watched her, her eyes narrowed. "You know," she started slowly. "If you want him to notice you, don't be there."

Maddie looked confused.

"While he's chewing gum," London continued, "he'll be consumed with thoughts of you: Where is she? Why isn't she here? Is she on a hot date?" London pointed a perfectly manicured finger at Maddie.

Maddie smiled and crossed her arms. "I never thought of that," she said slowly.

London nodded. "You may be book smart, but trust me on this. When it comes to things that truly matter, like dating, it's time for the pupil to become the pupee." She smiled and nodded knowingly.

Pupee? Maddie was pretty sure that word wasn't going to be found in any dictionary. But she had her expertise and London had hers. . . . She smiled. Maybe it was time for a little tutoring herself!

Chapter 4

The next day after school, Zack and Cody hung out in the school yard. But this time they were not alone. They had their own posse—a small one, perhaps—but it was a posse nonetheless. As they walked past Drew and his friends, to everyone's surprise Drew stopped. His crew, of course, did exactly what he did.

"Hey, clones," said Drew. "Is it true that you really live in the Tipton Hotel?"

"Yeah, our mom sings there," said Cody.

"And it makes your place look like a dump!" Max piped in, pointing at Drew.

"Yeah!" said Tapeworm, mimicking Max.

Drew ignored the two of them and continued. "And are there really hot babes serving ice cream by the pool?"

Cody held up three fingers. "Three flavors," he bragged.

Zack nodded. "And we're talking about the *girls*," he added.

Drew pulled the twins away from Max and Tapeworm. He wanted to talk to Zack and Cody privately. He clapped his hands together. "Maybe we'll come over and hang out," Drew said, as if he were doing them a favor. Which he kind of was.

"You want to hang out with *us*?" Cody said, stunned.

Zack jabbed his lame brother in the side. "Of course he does!" he said.

Drew put his arms around the twins' shoulders. "You know, I always liked you two," he said, as they walked together.

"No, you didn't," said Cody. Zack reached around Drew and smacked Cody in the head, then followed it up with a quick flick to the ear. They were in with the cool crowd! Was his lame brother going to ruin everything?

"Quit it," said Cody.

Max and Tapeworm watched in disbelief as the twins walked away. Had their new friends forgotten about them already?

❖❖❖

That afternoon at 3:44, Maddie ran through her mental checklist. Hair brushed? Check! Lip gloss applied? Check! At 3:45, she smiled a big smile, turned, and . . . there he was! Right on time! It was Lance the lifeguard, looking cute as ever in his dark green Tipton polo and his gleaming shark's tooth necklace.

"What's up?" said Lance. Then he frowned. "So, uh, where were you yesterday? 'Cause, like, I was here and you weren't."

"Oh, I was with—" Maddie started to explain. But then she remembered her conversation with London. What would London do? she wondered. And then, a picture of London appeared in her mind. *Be mysterious*, said the imaginary London. *Aloof. Torture him.*

"Someone," Maddie began. Lance leaned

forward. "Someone . . . else," she finished coyly.

"Really?" said Lance, disappointed. "Oh, so I guess that means you wouldn't want to go out sometime?"

London's advice went right out the window. "How about tonight?" Maddie said eagerly.

Suddenly, London reappeared in Maddie's mind. *Whatever you do, don't look eager,* the vision said.

Maddie turned to Lance. "Not that I'm eager," she informed him. She thought for a moment. "I'll check my calendar." She grabbed her date book, opened to a random page, barely glanced at it, and slammed it shut. "I'm free," she declared.

The image of London vanished. So much for playing hard to get!

"Excellent," said Lance. He pointed both

index fingers at her. "We'll have dinner at the seaport." He smiled and walked away.

Maddie sighed happily and watched him go, twirling her hair idly. She had a date!

She didn't even notice London coming up and leaning over the counter. And London was hard to miss in her pink newsboy cap, black T-shirt with pink flamingos, pink pants, and fluffy pink scarf. "Hey!" London said. She wasn't used to being ignored.

"Oh, hey, London," Maddie said. "Your advice actually worked!"

"Duh," said London, starting to walk away. Then she turned around. "What advice?"

"I got a date with Lance, the lifeguard!" Maddie could hardly contain herself.

London thought about this for a moment, then asked the most important question.

"So, what are you going to wear?"

Maddie obviously hadn't given this any thought. "I don't know, jeans?"

London rolled her eyes. "Why don't you wear a sack over your head that says LOSER? Come on, let's go to the boutique."

Chapter 5

Mr. Moseby watched the two girls from across the lobby. He knew that London plus boutique did not equal studying, so he was about to follow them, but at the very same moment he got distracted. That's because the Tipton Hotel was suddenly overrun with guests. Young guests. Nonpaying guests.

Mr. Moseby watched in disbelief as kids

started pouring in through the revolving doors. Even worse, they all made a beeline for the table in the lobby that had just been set up for afternoon tea!

Mr. Moseby was just about to kick out the little hooligans when he realized it was Cody, Zack, and about fifteen of their friends. It would be sixteen, except that Tapeworm, unfortunately, had gotten stuck in the revolving door and was having a terrible time freeing himself.

Drew surveyed the spread, nodding. "Not bad. Not bad at all. Check it out, crew. All this stuff is free."

There was a murmur of approval as the kids grabbed dainty tea sandwiches and delicate cookies and began stuffing their faces.

"Free for our guests who spend two thousand dollars a day," Mr. Moseby pointed out.

"Do you have any hummus?" asked Achmed, a kid with spiky black hair, as he took a bite out of a finger sandwich.

Mr. Moseby gave him a stern look.

He was about to say something more, but just then Tapeworm finally freed himself from the door and elbowed his way to the tea table. There was nothing left. He stared at the empty platters, disappointed. "Aww, who ate all the finger sandwiches?" he asked.

Drew stared at him. "Who invited Ringworm?"

"It's *Tape*worm," Tapeworm corrected.

Mr. Moseby had heard quite enough. "Whatever type of worm he is, please take him and the rest of your mongrel horde upstairs and out of sight."

"Come on, guys," said Cody. "Let's hit the pool!"

"Please don't run!" begged Mr. Moseby.

Run? What a great idea! The kids took off, knocking into Mr. Moseby, who spun around, landing neatly in Carey's arms.

Even from this most undignified of positions, Mr. Moseby managed to keep his composure. He looked up at his singer. "Ah, just the person I wanted to talk to," he said, giving her a withering look.

❖❖❖

The rooftop of the Tipton Hotel was kid paradise. There was a pool, a Jacuzzi, a snack shack, plenty of lounge chairs, free towels, and, of course, ice cream. Three kinds.

The kids were indeed in heaven. Zack lay on a lounge chair, his shades on, arms behind his head. Cody sat next to him, sipping a fruity red drink. Achmed cooled off by spritzing himself with water, and Drew sat back, getting his shoulders massaged.

"Thanks, honey," he told his masseuse. "You were right. I was tense."

A waitress put down a tray filled with dishes of ice cream.

Zack smiled. The pleasures of hotel living. "Four o'clock ice cream!" he exclaimed happily.

"Like clockwork," agreed Cody.

Drew grabbed a dish. "Maybe you guys aren't so lame after all," he admitted to the twins.

As the rest of Drew's posse all grabbed bowls, Zack pulled Cody aside. "Did you hear that?" he said to his brother eagerly. "We're in! We're not so lame!"

Even Cody was excited. "We've never been so popular," he said.

"Boy-oh-boy-oh-boy!" Tapeworm had

noticed the ice cream and rushed to make his way through the crowd. But he and Max were too late. It was all gone.

"Aww, who ate all the ice cream?" Tapeworm asked.

"Too late, Earthworm," said Drew with a nasty laugh.

Max had a suggestion. "Hey, let's all go in the Jacuzzi!"

She and Tapeworm headed over, but were quickly edged out by Drew and his crew. So were a couple of the grown-up guests of the hotel, who looked very unhappy.

But Max wasn't giving up so easily. "Guys, move over. Make some room," she said.

Drew sneered. "Sorry, the kiddie pool's over there," he said, pointing. His posse laughed.

Tapeworm sighed. "Great, first no finger sandwiches, and then no ice cream, and now this."

"They always have extra at the cabana," said Cody helpfully.

"All right!" said Tapeworm as he and Max took off.

"Better not be melted," said Max over her shoulder.

As soon as Max and Tapeworm were gone, Drew had an idea. "Hey, y'all, let's ditch the dweebs."

His posse, of course, were all in agreement. But Cody didn't think it was a good idea.

"You go ahead. I'll wait and tell them where we're going," he said.

Drew stared at Cody like he had three heads.

Zack laughed uncomfortably. "He's not clear on the whole 'ditch' concept," he explained.

Drew rolled his eyes and he and his posse

ran off. Zack spun around to face his brother. Sure it was rude to abandon their new friends, no matter how dweeby they were. But this was the Drew Crew, for goodness sake!

Zack looked his brother in the eye. "Look, we just got past lame," he told Cody. "Don't screw things up."

"But Mom says we're not supposed to give in to peer pressure," argued Cody.

"We're not," explained Zack. "We're just doing what everybody else is doing. Come on!"

Cody didn't like this one bit. "But it will hurt their feelings."

"No, it won't," Zack explained. "They're going to laugh." He paused for a moment, then added, "Eventually." He ran off after Drew. Cody took a deep breath and ran off after his brother.

Chapter 6

The next afternoon, the Tipton Hotel lobby was again packed with kids. They were lounging on sofas and hoarding platters of finger sandwiches, their feet up on tables. Zack and Cody's mom walked in and looked around. Then she went over to the twins.

"Hey, guys," she said.

"Hey," said Zack casually.

"Where are Max and Tapeworm?" she asked.

Cody winced, remembering yesterday's ditching. "Uh . . . they might not be here today," he said carefully.

Drew held up an empty tray. "Yo, Zack, we're out of finger sandwiches!" he called.

Carey looked around again. "Whoa, Zack. Are all these kids with you?" she wanted to know.

"Yeah, we're part of their posse," Zack said proudly, crossing his arms.

Carey was not impressed. "Guys, I told you to bring home a *couple* of friends, not the entire school." She looked around and saw Mr. Moseby, who was supervising Esteban changing a lightbulb, staring at the kids. "Moseby's going to blow his top. Fix it!" Carey demanded.

"Okay, Mom, we'll take care of it," said

Zack. Carey nodded and headed upstairs.

Zack turned to Cody. "You want to tell Drew not to invite any more of his friends over?"

"No, it's okay. You can do it," Cody replied, giving Zack a push.

"We probably don't have to say anything. How many more friends could he have?" Zack said. He laughed nervously.

Just then, ten more kids wandered into the Tipton lobby.

"Yo, yo! Guys! Over here!" called Drew. Apparently, Drew had an unlimited supply of friends!

Not knowing what to do, and knowing that Moseby was about to freak out, Zack yelled, "All right! First one to the game room gets free foosball all afternoon!"

The kids all rushed toward the elevator, bumping into Mr. Moseby. Mr. Moseby, in turn, knocked into the ladder that Esteban was standing on. The ladder went flying. Esteban blindly grabbed for anything to steady him—which just happened to be the hotel's crystal chandelier.

"Oh, my!" cried Mr. Moseby.

"Whoa!" shouted Esteban, as he began to swing across the hotel lobby. Moseby's eyes widened in horror as Esteban headed straight for the table with the vase on it. Moseby ran to protect it.

"Oh! No, no!" he shouted. "Watch the vase! Watch out for the guests!" He looked around wildly and saw guests staring at the scene, their mouths open in shock. "Oh! Everything's fine, go have a bite at the bar!" he yelled at them.

As he swung over the lobby, Esteban was panicking. "Somebody call my mother!" he shouted.

But Moseby only had eyes for the vase. "Watch the vase! Don't! The vase!" he cried.

Somehow, Esteban managed to avoid the vase. He did not, however, manage to avoid Mr. Moseby. He crashed down right on top of him. Esteban jumped to his feet.

"I am okay! I am fine! Nothing happened to me! I am okay!" Then he looked down and realized that Mr. Moseby had cushioned his fall. "You!" Esteban shouted. "You saved my life! Oh, Mr. Moseby!" He hoisted Mr. Moseby in the air, hugging him tightly. "Thank you for saving my life, Mr. Moseby! In my country, my life now belongs to you."

Mr. Moseby had had enough. "I want those kids out of here," he growled. "Anyone without a room key is on the street!"

Esteban thought about this for a moment. "Well, since my life now belongs to you, I must obey this harsh command." He saluted Mr. Moseby smartly.

❖❖❖

Maddie rang the bell to London's luxurious suite. London threw open the door, once again dressed in a fabulous pink outfit—pink necklace, pink-and-white-striped off-the-shoulder sweater, pink skirt, and pink boots.

"So? How did it go with the lifeguard?" London asked excitedly.

Maddie hesitated for a moment. "Well . . ." She didn't look very happy.

London was concerned. "What's the matter? Didn't he love your outfit?"

"Yeah," said Maddie with a sigh. "But I don't think it's going to work."

London was confused. "Why not? He

loved your outfit. What else could it be?"

"But I didn't like *him*," explained Maddie.

London had a one-track mind. "Didn't you like *his* outfit?" she asked.

"London!" Maddie cried in frustration. "It's not all about outfits. It's about the people inside them."

This was a new concept for London. "Huh?" she said.

Maddie began to pace the room as she explained. "He's really nice but . . . all he can talk about is water!" She plopped herself down on London's pink couch. "Swimming in water, diving in water, splashing in water . . . saltwater versus freshwater. After talking to him for an hour, I had to go so bad!"

Just then Maddie's cell phone rang. She looked down at the display. "Oh, no, it's him!" she cried, tossing the offending phone onto a pink armchair. She sat closer to London, as if this would protect her.

London knew exactly what needed to be done. "Dump him! Dump him like last month's shoes!" she declared.

Maddie shook her head. "But I don't want to hurt him."

London rolled her eyes. "Oh, so you're just going to marry him and live poolside with a bunch of boring lifeguard babies?"

Maddie considered this terrible future for a moment. "You're right. I have to end it." She answered her phone. "Hi, Lance. Oh, I missed you, too." She giggled. "Oh, really!" She covered the mouthpiece, then told London, who was right behind her, trying to listen in, "Apparently the pH balance in the pool is perfect." She rolled her eyes.

Maddie returned to her call. The doorbell rang, and London ran to the door. It was Mr. Moseby.

"London," said Mr. Moseby. "How's the studying going?"

"Fabulous," answered London. "Thanks for checking in." She tried to close the door on Mr. Moseby, but he pushed his way inside, just in time to hear Maddie say, "Yes, yes, I think Chlorine is a beautiful name for a girl." Then she made an *Is-this-for-real?* face.

Mr. Moseby frowned. "Is there *any* teaching going on here *at all*?"

London smiled. "Oh, of course." She pointed to herself. "I'm teaching Maddie valuable life skills."

"She's supposed to be tutoring *you*!" Mr. Moseby spluttered. Then he said the magic words: "Your father said that if you flunk out again, he's sending you to parochial school."

London stared at Mr. Moseby in disbelief.

"I think you should never do that in public,"
replied Zack. "Or in private," added Cody.

"Why don't you guys invite over some
friends from school?" Carey suggested.

Zack rolled his eyes when his mom suggested they invite some friends to the hotel. "Too bad we don't have any."

"Hey, you guys wanna come over to our house?" Zack asked his new classmates.

"Wow," Carey said after Max showed off some dance moves. "Can you show me how you do that?"

"Ooh, I have to get downstairs. He's probably there already," Maddie said.

Zack turned to Cody. "You want to tell Drew not to invite any more of his friends over?"

"So . . . we're friends again?"
Cody asked hopefully.

"You mean like . . . where Maddie goes?"

Mr. Moseby nodded.

"And I'd have to wear . . ." London took one horrified glance at Maddie's outfit—blue blouse, plaid tie, and plaid skirt—and let out a horrified gasp. "A uniform?!" She pointed at the offensive outfit.

"Mmmm-hmmm," said Mr. Moseby. He was finally making some headway with this girl! He left London's suite to let what he had said sink in.

Just then Maddie hung up her phone and turned to London, a look of dismay on her face. "I can't believe I made another date with him!" she moaned.

But London had other things on her mind. "I can't believe I might have to wear plaid!" she cried.

Maddie turned to London in desperation. "Teach me to be mean!" she begged.

London stared back at Maddie. "Teach me to be smart!" she wailed.

The two girls clutched at each other. "Help me!" they cried.

Chapter 7

Back in the game room, Zack was still trying to be optimistic as he and Cody surveyed the out-of-control crowd of kids. "Good turnout," he said. "All of the A-list kids are here."

Cody was a little more realistic. "Yeah, but do any of them even know your name?" he asked.

"Yeah," Zack insisted.

Just then, Achmed yelled out to him. "Hey, Jack. Give me a quarter!"

Zack handed Achmed a quarter, then turned to his brother. "See?" he bragged. "Off by one letter."

Cody sighed.

"Psst!" Zack and Cody turned around. Esteban had stuck his head into the room. "Zack, Cody, I need to speak with you," he called. He walked over to the twins.

"What's up, Esteban?" Cody asked.

"I have been given a terrible task," Esteban said sadly. "I have been ordered to rid the premises of children by Mr. Moseby. Now, I could disobey him, but Mr. Moseby reminds me of my father, who was also strict, demanding, ruthless, and mean." Esteban got choked up for a moment. "Oh, I miss my papa so much."

He looked away, overcome with emotion.

"It's okay," Cody said soothingly.

"I need a moment," replied Esteban. He walked across the room and rested his head on his arm.

The boys turned back to each other. "We can't ask them to leave, they're our friends," said Zack.

"Hey, Zeke!" Achmed shouted angrily. "This stupid machine keeps eating all my quarters!"

"I think *your friend* is talking to you, Zeke," Cody said sarcastically.

Zack was finally convinced. "You're right. We have to get rid of them. But how?"

"I know!" Cody had a sudden inspiration. He ran to the middle of the room and raised his arms. "Hey!" he yelled. "Free foot-long grinders at the Saint Mark's Hotel across the street!"

Free grinders! The kids made a beeline for the elevators.

"Excellent," said Zack approvingly. "I'll clear out the lobby; you get the rooftop."

Zack and Cody put their hands together and raised them. "Break!" they shouted.

❖❖❖

Maddie was on candy-counter duty when she spotted Lance heading her way, whistling a merry tune. She ducked behind the counter, pretending to look for something.

"Hey," Lance said. She was caught! Maddie stood up and gave the lifeguard a fake smile.

"So," Lance began, "for our date I was thinking we take a quick swim, hit the Jacuzzi, and then watch *Seabiscuit*."

He was obviously very proud of his plan.

Maddie gave Lance a look. "You do know it's about a horse," she said.

Lance looked puzzled. "A sea horse?" he asked uncertainly.

Maddie had had enough. "Lance, we need to talk." She walked out from behind the counter and stood next to him. "See, I think you're a really great guy and—"

Once again, imaginary London had something to say to Maddie. *Don't beat around the bush!* she insisted.

"The point is . . ." Maddie started firmly. But then she looked at Lance's confused expression and softened. "Life is like an ocean—it ebbs and flows —" She moved her arms from side to side to illustrate her point.

Imaginary London had clearly had enough. *Dump him now!* she insisted. *Don't make me come out of this bubble!*

Maddie spoke out loud to her imaginary friend. "Would you be quiet!" she said.

Now Lance was even more confused. "Who are you talking to?" he asked.

"No one," replied Maddie. She sighed and returned to her water metaphor. "Look, Lance . . . life is like a river—"

Lance leaned forward and smiled. "Actually, I prefer pools," he offered.

Enough was enough! "That does it!" Maddie said. "This isn't working. I can't go out with someone who only talks about water!"

Lance stared at Maddie. "*You're* the one who's talking about water," he said. "Sheesh." Looking hurt and a bit bewildered, he left the lobby.

Relieved, Maddie watched him go. Then London ran into the lobby, excitedly waving a piece of paper.

"Good news!" she cried.

"Me, too!" Maddie replied.

"Me first!" London said. "I got a D-plus in math!"

Maddie stared at London. "That's good news?" she asked.

"Yeah, thanks to you I passed! My daddy got me a plasma TV!"

Maddie shook her head. "Wow, when I get an A-plus, all I get is an extra slice of pie," she said.

London was puzzled. "Is that your good news?" she asked.

"No, no, no," explained Maddie. "I took your advice and broke up with Lance. I was blunt, I was direct, and if I say so myself, I was pretty darn mean!" she bragged.

"So I learned something from you, and you learned something from me!" London said proudly.

Maddie nodded. "Yeah. And now you have a plasma TV. . . ." A sudden realization dawned on her. "And I don't have a boyfriend," she finished sadly.

"So everybody's happy!" London said obliviously. She squealed and skipped out of the lobby, leaving Maddie slumped at the candy counter.

Maddie was well aware of the fact that life was sometimes not fair, but this was ridiculous!

Chapter 8

Meanwhile, Operation Get Rid of the Drew Crew was underway. The elevator doors slid open, and Zack popped out, looking furtive. "Go! Go! Go!" he said, motioning for the kids inside to leave. Last but not least was an elderly woman with a walker. She scurried out of the elevator under Zack's watchful eyes.

Cody had rooftop duty. He spotted a group of kids hanging out in the Jacuzzi.

"Hey, guys, you need to leave," Cody told them.

They merely glanced at him, then giggled and returned to their conversation. Thinking quickly, Cody grabbed a dish of chocolate ice cream and, when no one was looking, tossed it into the Jacuzzi.

"Ew, gross!" he cried, pointing.

Everyone leaped out of the Jacuzzi, squealing. Zack arrived, breathless. He stared at the ice cream and looked to Cody for an explanation.

"Don't ask," said Cody. "How are we doing?"

"I got rid of everybody downstairs," Zack explained. "Except one kid that was crying and begging to stay." He winced. "Turns out his parents are actually guests here."

There was just one thing left to do—get rid of the Drew Crew. This was going to be tough. He and his original gang were playing basketball.

"Drew!" called Cody. "Drew! Listen, Drew! Drew!" Drew ignored him. "We need to talk to you!" Cody said.

"What?!" Drew said, annoyed.

"Take it away, Zack," said Cody, pushing Zack forward.

"You see," Zack began nervously. "The thing is, we kind of need you to leave."

"We're in the middle of a game," Drew said dismissively.

Cody couldn't take it anymore. He pushed Zack behind him.

"No. That doesn't work for us," he said firmly. "You need to leave." Drew stepped forward and Cody immediately backed down. "Tell him why, Zack," he said.

Zack glared at Cody.

"Man, you guys need to chill," Drew said. "'Cause if we leave, we're not coming back. Then you'll have to hang with those two dweebs, Max and Silkworm."

Max and Tapeworm had just arrived on the rooftop and were standing by the door. They could hear everything.

"His name is *Tape*worm," said Zack. "And he's our friend." Max and Tapeworm smiled at each other. Then he added, "And so is the other dweeb." This time Max and Tapeworm did not look so happy.

"Yeah!" Cody said. "And they liked us before they knew we had this cool place and dainty finger sandwiches."

"That's right," added Zack. "And then you made us ditch them." He thought for a moment. "You know what, now we're ditching you. Give me back the ball."

"Fine," said Drew angrily. "Here." He threw the ball backward over his head. It flew across the roof and slammed into a satellite dish, showering sparks everywhere and knocking the dish off the roof. The cable that the dish was attached to began to strain under the sudden weight, and the metal brackets holding it down began to pop off one by one. Drew and his crew panicked and ran away. The twins gasped and grabbed the cable. But how long could they hold on?

Downstairs, the boys' mother had just gotten off the elevator and was walking across the lobby when Mr. Moseby stopped her.

"Ms. Martin, I want you to know I had to use hotel staff to round up the rabble your children unleashed on this hotel," he told her.

Carey rolled her eyes. "Mr. Moseby," she began, "every little problem with you is like

Chapter 9

On the roof, Zack and Cody held on for dear life to the end of the satellite cable. They were desperately trying to pull the dish back up where it belonged.

"I can't believe we broke the hotel," said Zack. They hauled the cable over their shoulders, groaning as they pulled.

Suddenly, a familiar voice spoke. "It looks

like you could use some help," it said.

Cody and Zack turned around to see Max and Tapeworm standing there.

"What are you guys doing here?" asked Zack.

"Well, we came here to tell you off," said Tapeworm.

"But lucky for you, we overheard you guys defending us 'dweebs,'" finished Max.

"Sorry we ditched you," said Zack, shamefaced.

"So . . . we're friends again?" Cody asked hopefully.

Max looked at Tapeworm. "We'll have to think about it," she answered.

Suddenly, the weight of the dangling satellite dish shifted, and Zack and Cody were yanked against the wall.

"Could you think fast," Zack begged, "because I think I just caught a bus!"

Max and Tapeworm decided the twins had suffered enough.

"Okay," said Tapeworm.

The two friends grabbed the end of the cable, and they all began to pull. Just at that moment, Zack and Cody's mother arrived. She couldn't believe her eyes!

"What have you done?" she cried, startling her sons.

"Mom!" they shouted, letting go of the cable. Max and Tapeworm were jerked toward the edge of the roof.

Carey shook her head in disbelief. "I'm surprised at you two!" she said. Then she looked at Max and Tapeworm. "And you two, too!" she added.

"They didn't do it," Zack explained.

"They were the only two that stayed to help," Cody said.

Meanwhile, Max and Tapeworm were

slowly losing their grip. "Guys! Come on!" they shouted.

Zack, Cody, and their mom rushed over and grabbed the end of the cable line.

As they pulled, Zack continued to explain. "It wasn't us," he told his mother. "It was that kid, Drew." He turned around to address his twin. "I told you he was no good."

Cody had completely lost his patience with his brother by then. "You. Said. Nothing," he said in a low and angry voice.

"I don't care who did it," said Carey. "Pull! It's still your responsibility. Pull! When I told you this hotel is your home, I meant you should treat it with respect. Pull!"

"Sorry. I guess I messed up," Zack admitted.

"Zack's right," Cody added. "He messed

up." Zack gave him a dirty look. "Pull!" Cody yelled at him.

Just then, a waitress walked by with a tray full of ice cream.

"Ooh, four o'clock ice cream!" Tapeworm shouted.

Lured by the frosty, mouthwatering treat, the four kids let go of the cable at the same time. Carey was left alone, holding the cable and supporting the entire weight of the satellite dish. She struggled to maintain her grip, and was dragged to the wall. She planted her feet against it and held on tight.

"Guys?" she asked. "Guys! Aw, come on! Help!" She shook her head. "Oh man, I picked the wrong day to wear heels!" she said.

❖❖❖

Later that afternoon, after the satellite dish was returned to its rightful place, Max and Tapeworm sat on lounge chairs, sunning themselves. Mr. Moseby stood nearby.

Max looked up. "You know, Moseby, you run a nice place around here," she said appreciatively.

Mr. Moseby nodded. "Thanks, son," he said.

"I'm a girl!" cried Max.

Meanwhile, Cody and Zack were busy scrubbing the Jacuzzi. They wore snorkel masks and had toothbrushes in their hands.

"This is the worst punishment we ever got," said Cody.

"I think we scrubbed every single tile," Zack complained, looking at his wrinkled, pruny fingertips.

"I can't uncurl my fingers," added Cody.

Carey ran onto the roof, looking excited.

"Hey, Max, I finally learned that move!" she cried, starting to dance. Max got up and joined her.

The boys watched, thoroughly embarrassed.

"I don't know her," said Cody.

"Neither do I," replied Zack.

Too mortified to watch, the twins ducked underwater, making a huge splash. And Mr. Moseby, who was standing nearby, got completely soaked.

It was turning into just another normal day for the twins. After all, there hadn't been a dull moment at the Tipton Hotel since they had moved in!

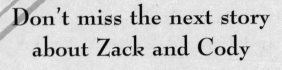

Don't miss the next story about Zack and Cody

Adapted by N.B. Grace

Based on the television series, "The Suite Life of Zack & Cody", created by Danny Kallis & Jim Geoghan

Based on the episode written by Danny Kallis & Jim Geoghan

The Tipton Hotel lobby was bustling: rich and famous guests were checking in, rich and famous guests were checking out, and hotel employees were running around taking care of them all. As usual, Mr. Moseby, the hotel manager, was stationed behind the front desk, keeping a careful eye on everything.

Two preppy teenage boys, carrying sports-equipment bags, entered the lobby. They dropped their bags against the front desk, startling Mr. Moseby.

"Hey, man," one of the boys said to Mr. Moseby.

"Yo, dudes," Mr. Moseby replied with a big smile, doing his best to sound hip.

But Mr. Moseby had a long way to go before he could ever be considered hip. He was wearing an elegant gray suit and a spotless tie. He simply did not look like someone who would use the word "dudes."

The two boys looked at each other, then shrugged. As long as Mr. Moseby could check them into their rooms, who cared what he called them?

Across the lobby, London Tipton, the daughter of the hotel's wealthy owner, was leaning against the candy counter. She was busy congratulating herself on the super-fashionable outfit she had thrown together that morning: a gray fedora hat, a black-and-silver tank top, a short skirt, and pink pearls.

And now that she had spotted the two new hotel guests, she was even happier about her outfit.

"Mmm-mmm," she purred to Cody and Zack Martin, the twelve-year-old twins who were manning the candy counter. "Look what the hunk fairy just dropped off. Jason Harrington and Kyle Lawford." She snapped her fingers at Zack and Cody. "Gloss me!" she commanded.

"Sorry, we're watching the counter for Maddie," Zack said. "And we're not allowed to accept money, make change, or touch any of the merchandise." *Especially* not the lip gloss, he thought with disdain.

"Is there anything you *can* do?" she pouted.

"I can shove twelve gummy worms up my nose," Cody said brightly. "Wanna see?"

London made a face just as Maddie Fitzpatrick, a hotel employee, breezed into the lobby, wearing a miniskirt, a green sweater, a pink-striped blouse, and boots. She looks nice enough, London thought to herself, but not as stylish as me—not by a long shot!

"Where have you been?" London barked. "Never mind." She snapped her fingers. "Gloss me, candy girl."

Maddie snapped her fingers back. "Off the clock," she said easily. London could be difficult, but Maddie knew how to handle her. Maddie smiled at Zack and Cody. "Thanks, guys."

"No problem, sweet thang," Zack said. He had heard an actor use the line on a late-night TV show, and the girl he had used it on had fallen in love with him by the first commercial break. Zack had memorized the line and practiced using it for a moment just like this.

But Maddie said, very nicely, "Awww. Call me in ten years."

Zack's face fell. Apparently, flirting is harder than it looks on TV, he thought to himself.

Maddie checked her watch. "If I hurry, I can make family night at Buffet Town," she said, adding, "it's my turn to pretend it's my birthday."

London sighed. For some reason, Maddie seemed to like chain restaurants and special menu deals. It was so *not rich* of her!

Speaking of rich . . . London thought, as Kyle and Jason walked toward her.

"London?" Kyle asked. "Hey, London!"

"Kyle! Small world," she said as casually as she could.

Jason was staring at Maddie, clearly smitten. "Hi," he said to her. "I'm Jason."

Maddie stared back. "I'm . . . uh . . . uh . . ." she started.

"Maddie," Cody said helpfully.

Maddie nodded, still staring into Jason's gorgeous eyes. "What he said," she said.

"You come to the Tipton Hotel often?" Jason asked.

Maddie blinked. Jason must have thought she was a guest at the hotel. As if she would ever have enough money to pay for a room at the Tipton Hotel!

Still, she thought, why not play along? She nodded. "Constantly. It's like I live here." Which, she thought, wasn't *exactly* a lie. . . . She did work really long hours.

Well, this is cute, London thought, as she

watched Maddie fall head over heels right in front of her. But let's get the focus back on *me*! "So, Kyle," she said, batting her eyes. "You in town for the Usher concert?"

"Semester break," Kyle explained. "Our parents arrive from Aspen tomorrow. Then we fly to Bermuda." He shrugged. "Our moms lost their tans skiing."

Maddie's eyes widened at the thought of flying to Bermuda after a ski vacation just so you could get your tan back. "Oh, I hate when that happens," she said.

Maddie checked her watch again. "Well, as we say, gotta jet," she said. She turned to Jason and smiled. "Nice to meet you."

As Maddie walked toward the door, Zack ran after her. "You don't really like that guy, do you?" he asked.

Maddie glanced back at Jason and shrugged. "He's cute," she admitted, "but

I've worked here long enough to know his type. Rich people don't care about anything but themselves."

They both watched as Kyle started to throw his soda can into the garbage. Jason grabbed the can from him and said, "Whoa, hey, man, recycle that!"

"Are you serious?" Kyle asked.

Maddie ran back toward Jason. "You recycle?" she asked.

"Sure," Jason nodded. "Cans, bottles, newspapers."

Maddie's eyes narrowed. Was he for real, she wondered, or just trying to make himself look good? "Since when?" she asked.

Jason laughed a little. "Since my father bought Oregon and started chopping down the trees," he admitted. "Have you heard of Opticorp?"

Maddie gasped. "The center of all evil?"

"That's Dad," Jason said ruefully.

Maddie couldn't believe it. "I protested against them!" she told Jason.

"Me, too!" he said excitedly.

"I got dragged off by a cop!" Maddie added.

"I got grounded for two weeks!" Jason countered.

Hmmm, London thought. Sparks really seem to fly when people talk about recycling. Well, she had never been much of an eco-freak, but it might be worth a try. . . .

She turned to Kyle. "I recycle, too."

"Really?" Kyle looked doubtful.

London nodded eagerly and twirled the strands of her pink pearl necklace. "I wore these pearls yesterday!" she explained.

Kyle smiled. London may not really understand the concept of recycling, he thought, but she's a lot of fun.